ANTICUCHO
& OTHER PERUVIAN CYBERPUNK STORIES

CREATED BY **GUSTAFFO VARGAS**
COLOUR FLATS **LAURA DRAGON**
ENGLISH LANGUAGE ADAPTATION **FRASER CAMPBELL**
ENGLISH PROOF READING **TOM WOOLNOUGH**
SPANISH PROOF READING **GAB CONTRERAS**

First Printing 2024 by Comic Printing UK

tacu tinta **PRESS**

www.gustaffovargas.com

TAYTA UKUKU

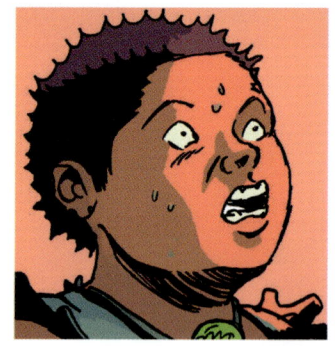

DON'T LIE TO ME, **PORK CHOP**.

ARE YOU KIDDING YOURSELF YOU'RE SOME KIND OF NINJA?

BUAAAAAA, NNOOO, PLEASE DON'T **HURT** ME, I'M SO HUNGRY, AND MY MA' IS SICK AT THE HOSP--

GULP!

YOU LYING PIGGY.

GGMMPFFF!

LET'S FIND OUT HOW TASTY THIS PIGGY IS, HEH?

WE'RE GOING TO SLICE YOU UP AND **COOK** YOU, PORKY.

IT'S NO USE. HE'S ALREADY IN **UKUKU** TERRITORY.

IF WE TRY TO GET INSIDE THEIR **TURF**, THEY'LL SEE US COMING FROM MILES AWAY.

GODDAMNED **LIMÓN**! HOW MANY TIMES HAVE I TOLD HIM TO STOP DOING STUPID SHIT!

HE'S SO PIG-HEADED!

LIMÓN WAS NICKING ONE OF THEIR **VARAYOCS**, THAT'S WHEN THEY GOT HIM.

THEY TOLD HIM THEY WERE GOING TO COOK HIM UP.

IS IT TRUE THAT THE **UKUKUS COOK** THEIR **ENEMIES**?

I DON'T KNOW AND I DON'T WANT TO FIND OUT, **MACACO**.

TSSS...

C'MON, THINK, THINK.

ÑUCO, LOOK FOR **ZANAHORIA!** HE MIGHT HAVE SOMETHING WE CAN USE.

I'LL CHECK WITH **LA SEÑO**.

GOTCHA.

EVERYBODY! LOOK FOR ANYTHING WE CAN USE TO MAKE A **DEAL!**

BUT, TELL ME FIRST!

COME ON, **MOVE!!!**

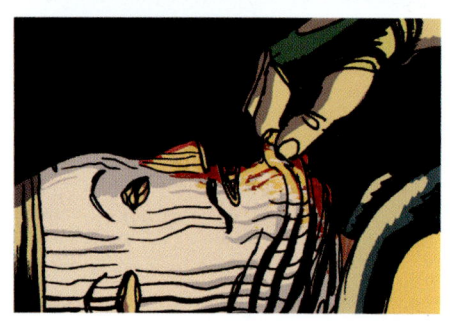

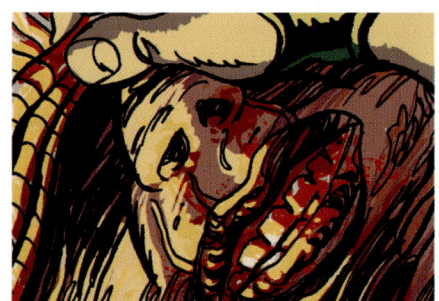

ANAQ IS STILL PASSED OUT. HIGH AS A KITE. HIS BODY IS FULL OF SOME KIND OF PSYCHNEURO.

AN UKUKU USING ORGANICS IN A FIGHT?

DON'T THINK SO. LOOKS LIKE ANAQ **HIT HIM** REALLY HARD.

THE **GALLINAZOS** WERE LACED UP AND WE HAVE NO EYES ON THE SCENE.

SOMEBODY IS **HIDING** THE UKUKU.

SHAKE THE STREETS AND BRING HIM TO ME.

THE AIR FEELS HEAVIER.

WE'RE DEFINITELY GETTING **CLOSER**.

YEAH, WE'VE HAD **EYES** ON OUR NECKS FOR A WHILE.

IF WE'D MADE IT THIS FAR, IT'S BECAUSE THEY'VE GOTTEN **CURIOUS**.

THEY KNOW WE'RE HERE FOR **LIMON**.

THEY'RE WONDERING WHAT WE HAVE TO **TRADE**.

THAT. OR IT'S A **TRAP**.

THIS IS AS FAR AS YOU GET.

UFFF...

BRING THE PORK CHOP.

LILAAA...!!! SNIFF SNIFFFF!

WHAT TOOK YOU SO LONG?

THEY'RE BULLIES!

CALM DOWN. IT'S ALL GOOD NOW. ALL GOOD.

SNIFF SNIFFFF.

GIRL. WAIT UP.

THERE'S SOMETHING ELSE.

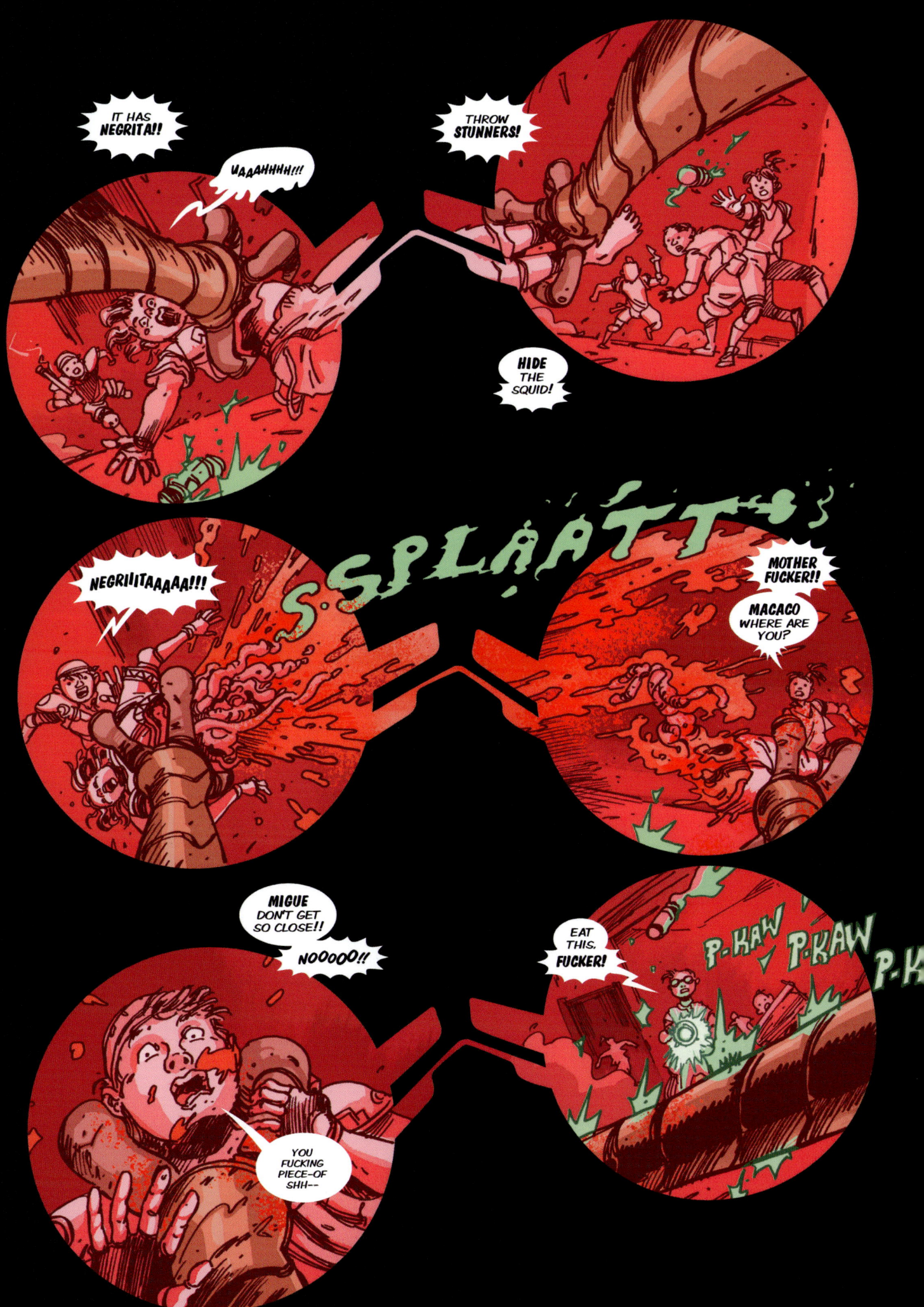

COME ON ANITA. WE NEED SOME GOOD NEWS HERE.
THIS DAY'S BEEN THE FUCKING WORST.
WELL, LIMÓN'S NOT EXACTLY POISONED, BUT THERE'S A LOT HAPPENING INSIDE HIM.
HIS ENTIRE ORGANISM IS BEING AFECTED BY THE SQUID.
IT'S LIKE THERE'S A BATTLE GOING ON INSIDE.
TACUCHI

I'VE GIVEN HIM A HEAVY DRUG COCKTAIL.
HE'S IN A MILD COMA, SO HE'S NOT SUFFERING.
I HAVE NO IDEA WHAT THAT SQUID'S DOING TO HIM.
AS I SAID, THERE'S A GREAT DEAL OF ACTIVITY.
ONLY THING WE CAN DO NOW IS KEEP MONITORING HIM.
IF HIS VITALS GET TOO LOW, CALL ME AND I'LL COME DOWN.

DAY 1

DAY 2

DAY 3

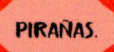

PIRAÑAS.

JUST A PACK OF STINKING KIDS.

FIRST, YOU DISRUPT MY SACRED TRANSCENDENCE.

AND NOW YOU LITTLE SHITS BRING THESE LOSERS AND ATTACK OUR SACRED PLACE.

DON'T YOU WORRY, I WILL NOT KILL YOU.

BUT I ASSURE YOU THAT YOU WILL LOSE YOUR SENSES FROM THE PAIN THAT I WILL BRING UNTO YOU.

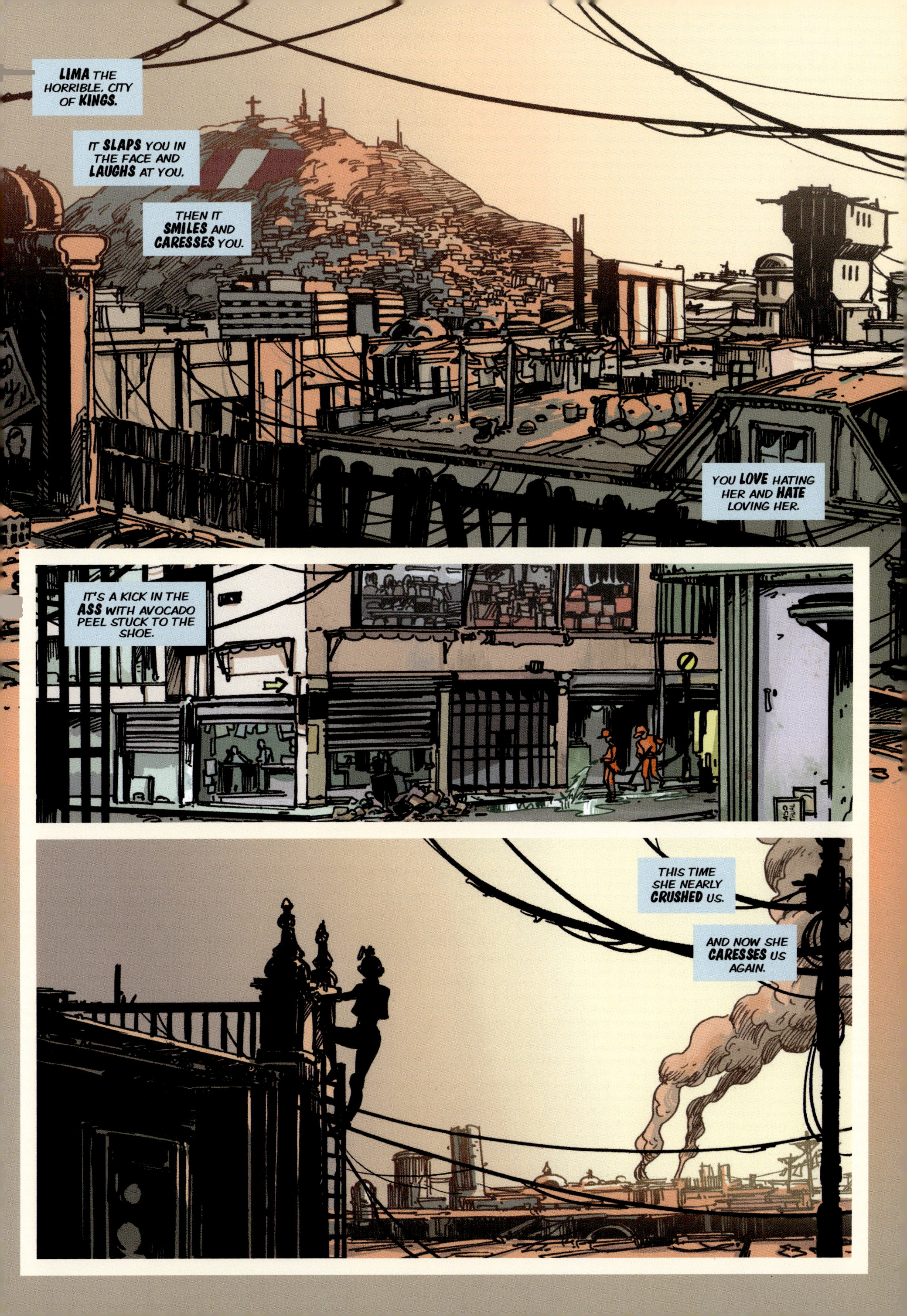

SHE'S MADE US KINGS.

LIMÓN WON'T SAY WHAT THE SQUID WAS...

...ONLY THING WE KNOW IS THAT IT WAS DESTINED FOR THE CHAVÍN PRIEST.

LIMÓN'S STUPIDITY ENABLED HIS TRANSCENDENCE.

HE WASN'T POISONED OR DYING

HE WAS BEING CHANGED, UPGRADED.

LIMÓN IS NOT LIMÓN ANYMORE.

NOW WE HAVE OUR OWN GOD.

A TECH-GOD

ONE THAT CONTROLS ALL TECHNOLOGY AROUND HIM.

Patasca

Carapulcra

Cau Cau

Arroz con Pollo + Huancaína

Lomo
Saltado

Tacu
Tacu

Ají de Gallina

Seco
de Res

**Papa
Rellena**

Arroz con Leche
+
Mazamorra Morada

Picarones

Choclo
con
Queso

Pancita

Chicha Morada

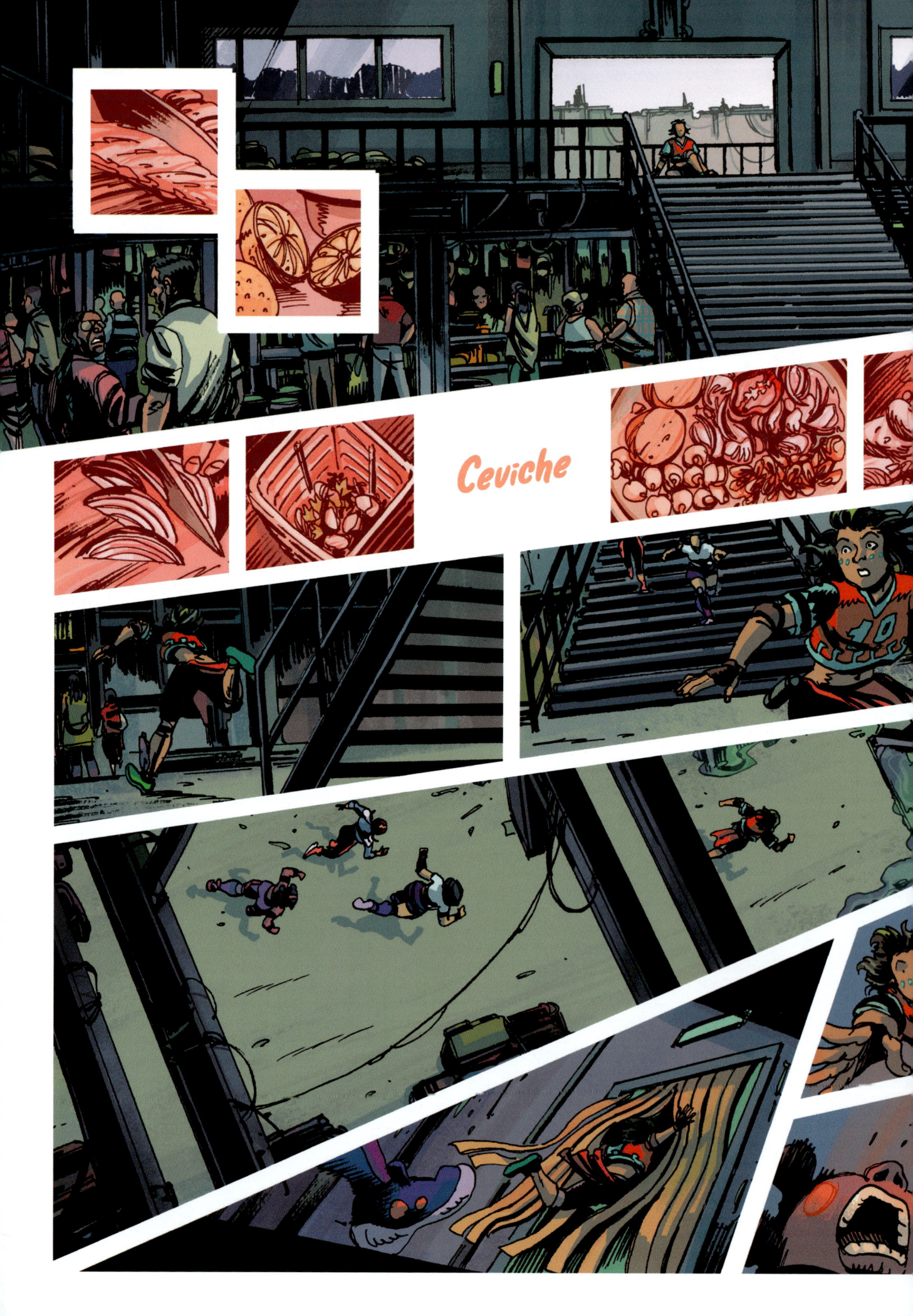

Ceviche

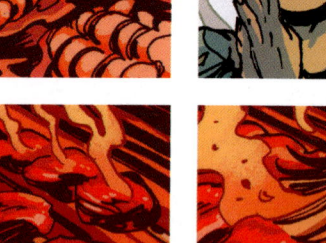

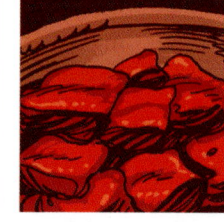

Anticucho!

CHARACTER DESIGN & WORLD BUILDING

Back in 2018, I wanted to tell a story with streets kids and gallinazos taking place in Lima, my city.

Lima is on the Peruvian coast, a warm and humid city where it almost never rains, their rooftops are filled with clutter and old things. The piraña gang using these rooftops to move through the city was a perfect fit.

Early Piraña sketches.

PIRAÑAS

These characters took a lot of research and sketching. I already knew that Lila and Limón were essential to telling the story, but I still didn't know how strong their relationship would be.

LILA

LIMÓN

CHABUCA

LALO

MIGUELITO

ÑUCO

ANITA ZANAHORIA

SECONDARY CHARACTERS

Cyberpunk worlds are filled with characters that add vital background.

Anita is an underground medic, Zanahoria is a resourceful hacker. For Tayta Ukuku I added Chicharrón, the 'fish' dealer and Chicho, the loader.

CHICHARRÓN CHICHO

MAGO NEGRITA PANCHITO MACACO CHINO

SACERDOTE CHAVÍN

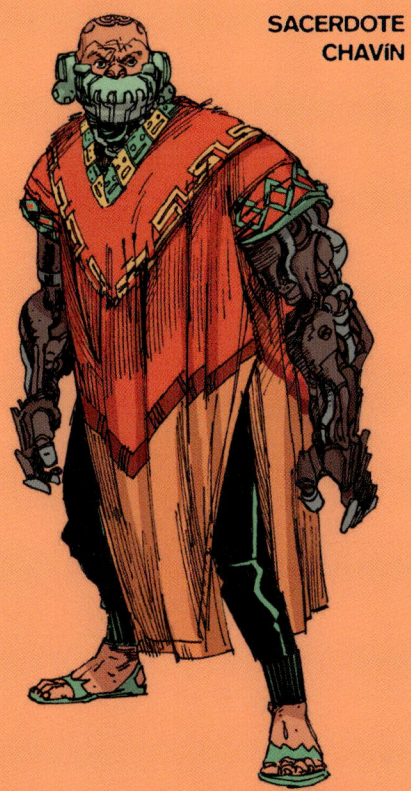

LOS CHAVINES

This gang is directly influenced by the Pre-Incan Culture Chavín de Huantar. They take ancient rituals from their ancestors and mix them with cyborg and bio technologies.

Sacerdote concept sketches.

HUANCA

SACERDOTISA

JAGUAR   **DRAGÓN**

I designed Dragón and Jaguar together, their fight would be messy and to the death. They needed to be easily distinguishable from one another.

GALLINAZOS

These curious carrion birds are spread over the city of Lima and a good part of the coast of Perú.

Using them as cyborg drones made perfect sense to the world building.

Although we see only these Chavines characters briefly, it was very important to establish a strong presence of crime and violence around them.

CABEZA CLAVA

The Cabeza Clavas are one of the most popular examples of Chavín de Huantar art.

This character took a while to develop, started as a cyborg, then bio-modified warrior, humanoid robot and in the end I kept the essence: a menacing head with legs.

TAYTA
UKUKU

DOLOR
EXTREMO

UKUKU CLAN

The first fight in L1MA was originally going to be a Chavín against an Ukuku, instead of a Dragón. Later I decided to use the Ukukus in the final sequence, in a big battle with the Chavines.

In the end I decided starting the sequence with that gory image, giving a stronger impact than the fight itself. I've been looking to revisit these characters for a good while.

DIABLO

MORE CHAVINES

My original plan was to use previous Chavín characters from L1MA, like the regular soldiers, and even Sacerdotisa or Huanca. But the tempation to design new characters was too strong!

ANAQ

LAS CHAPOSAS

To keep up the chase in the foreground, I needed a similar antagonist gang to the Pirañas, a group that would keep up their same pace, and so Las Chaposas entered the game.

The idea to portray Peruvian food in Lima, which comes from all the regions of Perú, has been roaming my head for years. ANTICUCHO is my excuse to show the many delicious varieties of Peruvian food.

Food is culture and character, it carries history and gives us meaning and identity. It's the celebration of our origins and its mix with other cultures. In Lima, if you run into someone you always ask: 'what did you have for lunch?', their reply is followed by an 'ufff, so good!', and a conversation about favourite dishes begins.

LAYOUTS & COLOUR NARRATIVE

Any comic project involves many hours of planning, sketching and designing. ANTICUCHO story is probably the most time I've spent in the layout-thumbnail-sketch stage.

I draw very small pre-thumbnail sketches before the actual thumbnails, and keep on adjusting details. Many iterations were done, especially for the double page spreads that carry a lot of information.

MINI PRE-THUMBNAILS

PAGE SPREAD 4-5
PRE-THUMBNAILS ITERATIONS

PAGES 4 & 5 PENCILS

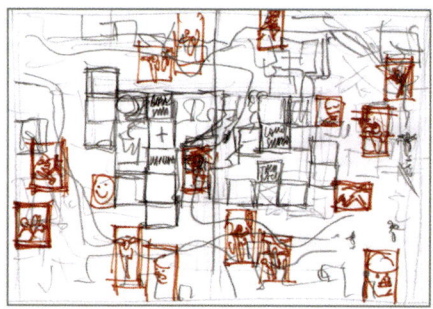

PAGES SPREAD 12-13 & 14-15 THUMBNAILS

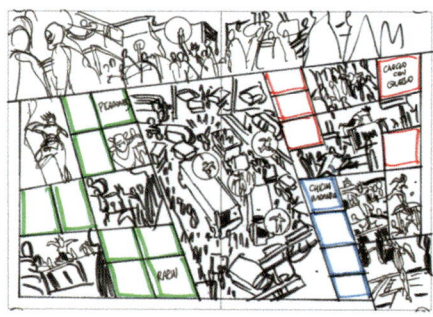

After the inking stage I usually do rough colours, laying all the pages together in a big canvas, to have control of the colour tones and rhythm.

To make sure that the chase sequences wouldn't clash with the food panels, I did the colour stage over the thumbnails and then went back to fixing and adjusting thumbnails.

A very laborious process, but I guess the result was worth the headache. :D

PAGES SPREAD 12-13 & 14-15 ROUGH COLOUR OVER THUMBNAILS

PIN-UP
GALLERY

Joe Palmer • CHAPOSAS

Linnea Sterte • BIGOTE

Gustaffo Vargas • L1MA COVER